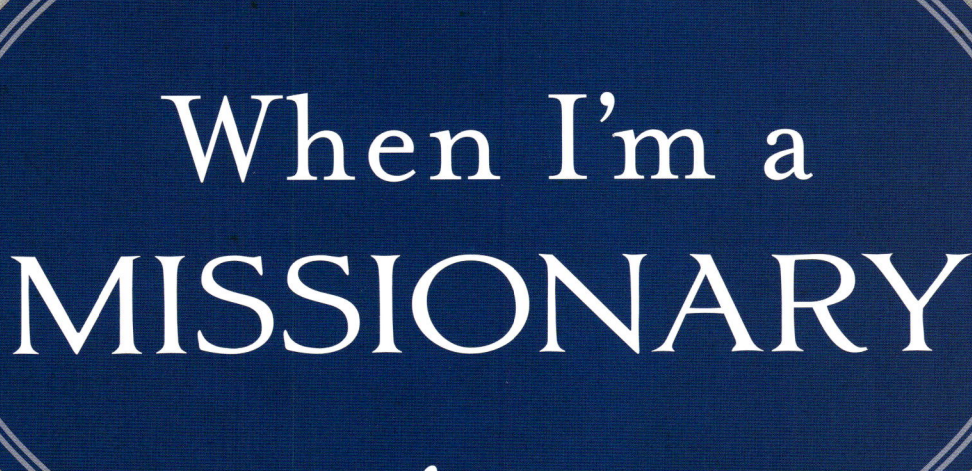

MERRILEE BOYACK
Illustrated by BRIAN CALL

DESERET BOOK

SALT LAKE CITY, UTAH

*To my dear husband, Steve, who served a
mission in Chile and blazed the trail for our family.*
—M.B.

*To Natalie, my first missionary, and to Kyle and Breanne, my
future missionaries, who helped me so much with this book.*
—B.C.

Text © 2015 Merrilee Boyack
Illustrations © 2015 Brian Call

Illustrations of Book of Mormon cover (pp. 10, 18), *Preach My Gospel* cover (p. 18), and Spanish missionary name tag (p. 24) by Brian Call © Intellectual Reserve, Inc.

All rights reserved. No part of this book may be reproduced in any form or by any means without permission in writing from the publisher, Deseret Book Company, P. O. Box 30178, Salt Lake City, Utah 84130. This work is not an official publication of The Church of Jesus Christ of Latter-day Saints. The views expressed herein are the responsibility of the author and do not necessarily represent the position of the Church or of Deseret Book Company.

All characters in this book are fictitious or are portrayed fictitiously. Any resemblance to actual persons, living or dead, is purely coincidental.

DESERET BOOK is a registered trademark of Deseret Book Company.

Visit us at DeseretBook.com

Library of Congress Cataloging-in-Publication Data

Boyack, Merrilee Browne, author.
 When I'm a missionary / Merrilee Boyack ; illustrations by Brian Call.
    pages cm
  ISBN 978-1-62972-100-2 (hardbound : alk. paper)
 1. Missions—Fiction. 2. Brothers and sisters—Fiction. 3. Mormons—Fiction. 4. The Church of Jesus Christ of Latter-day Saints—Missions—Fiction. I. Call, Brian D., illustrator. II. Title.
PZ7.1.B69Iam 2015
 [E]—dc23   2015012426

Printed in China   5/2015
RR Donnelley, Shenzhen, China

10 9 8 7 6 5 4 3 2 1

Lacey and Julian jumped up and down. They were excited to see their older brother, Elliott, who was coming home from his mission.

He scooped them up in his arms. "Who are these big kids?" he teased. "You've grown so much, I didn't even recognize you!"

"I'm going to be a missionary when I grow up!" Lacey exclaimed. "Me too!" Julian said. "Will you teach us how?"

"You bet!" Elliott said. "You'll both be great missionaries."

On Sunday, Julian put on his white shirt and tie to go to church. Lacey wore a cute blouse and skirt.

"Look, I'm dressed like a missionary!" Lacey said.

"I look like a missionary too!" Julian said.

When they got to church, Lacey and Julian ran to see the missionaries. "Look at us!" they said. "We look like missionaries!"

The two missionaries shook their hands. "You do!" they said.

"I'm going to be a missionary when I grow up," Julian said.

"It's good practice to dress like a missionary when you come to church," the tall elder said.

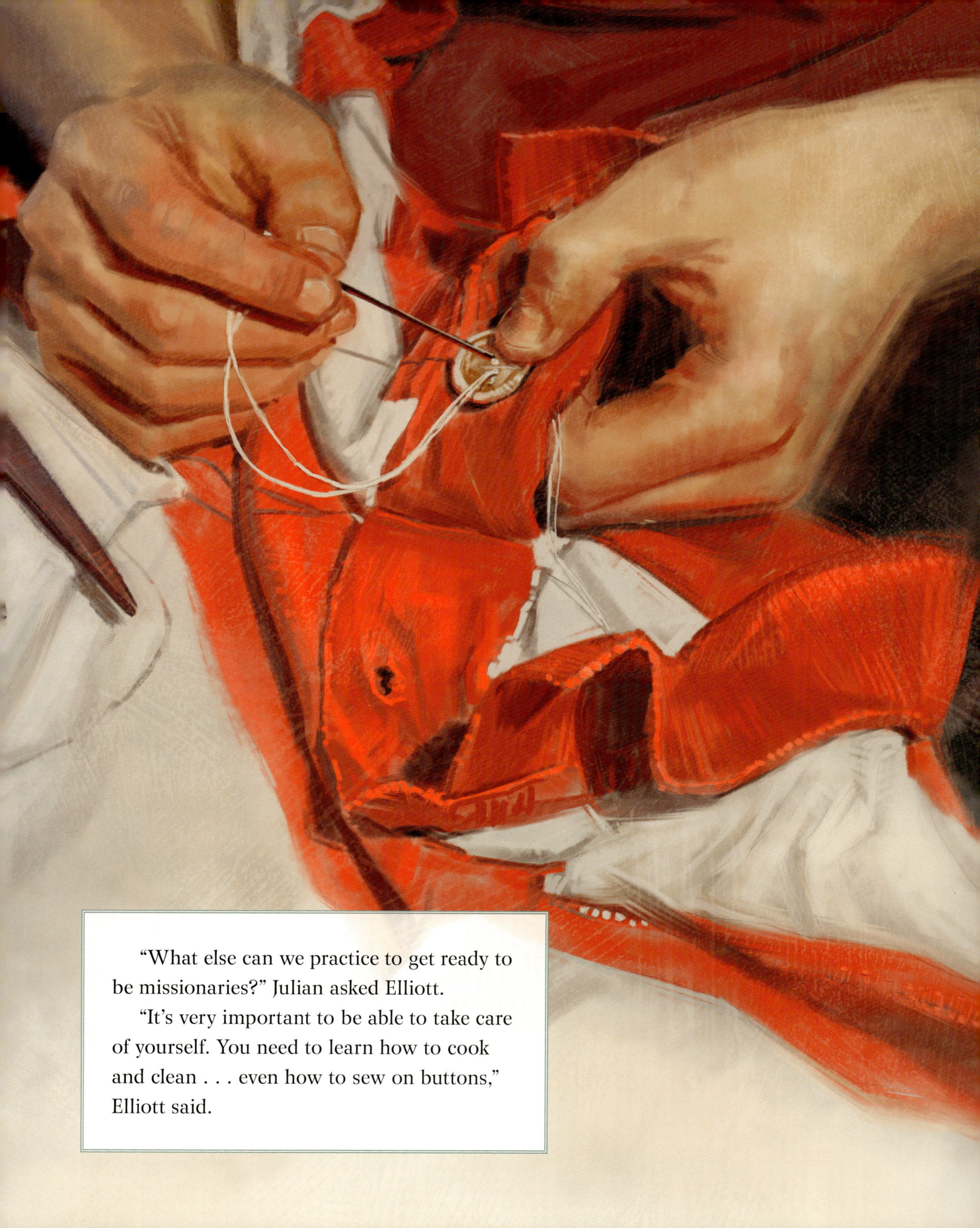

"What else can we practice to get ready to be missionaries?" Julian asked Elliott.

"It's very important to be able to take care of yourself. You need to learn how to cook and clean . . . even how to sew on buttons," Elliott said.

Julian and Lacey learned a lot that week. They cleaned their rooms and made their beds. Dad taught them how to make a sandwich and cook soup. Mom even taught them how to iron their clothes.

"Wow!" Mom said. "You are going to be really prepared to be missionaries when you're older. Keep learning and you'll be ready."

On Saturday, Julian and Lacey's grandpa came to visit. "Hi, Grandpa," Julian said. "We're learning how to be good missionaries!"

"That's a wonderful thing," Grandpa said. "I brought something to show you. These are my scriptures from when I was a missionary. Do you have your scriptures?"

"Yes, we do!" they said, and they ran to their bedrooms to get them.

"Look, Grandpa, here are my first scriptures," Lacey said.

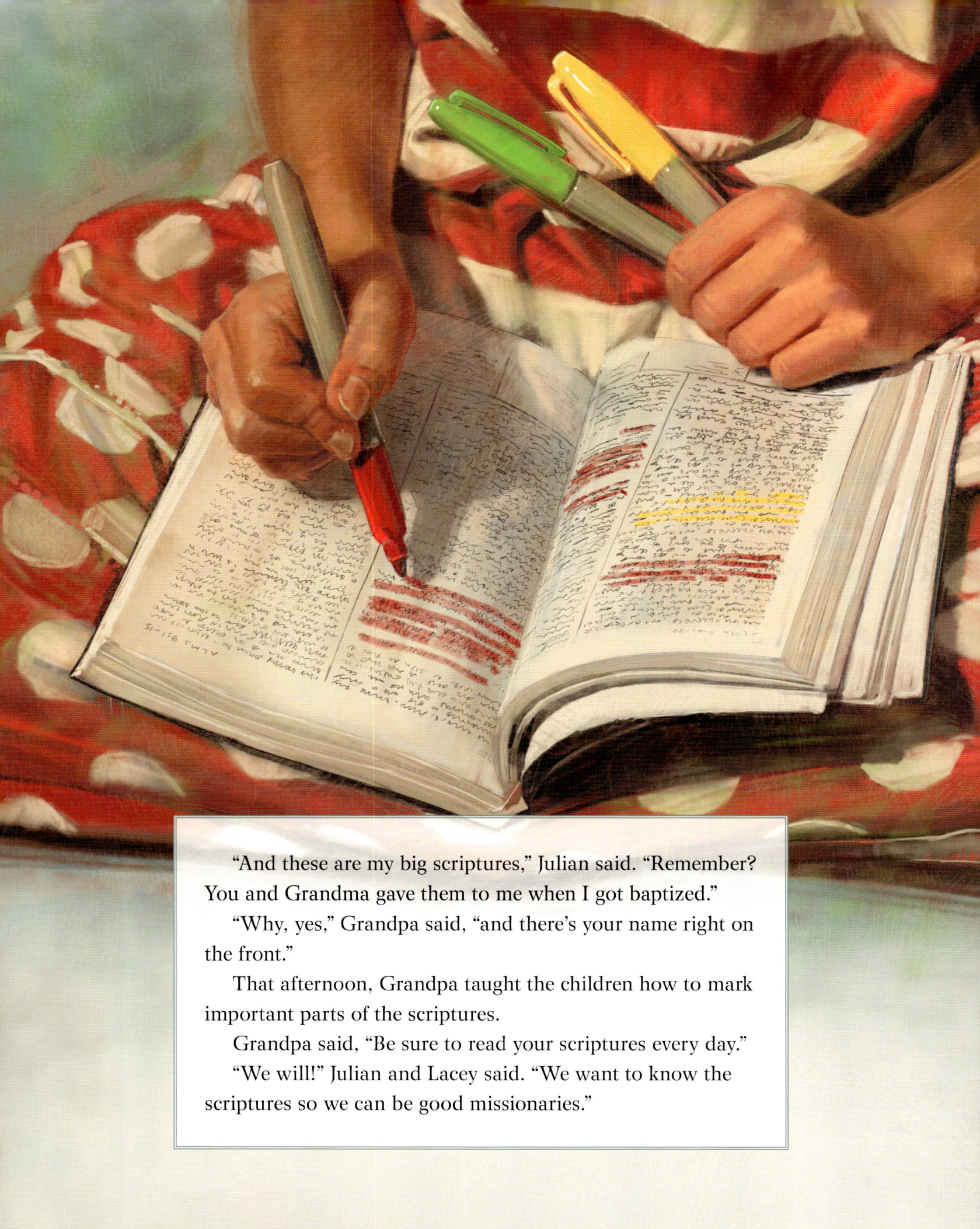

"And these are my big scriptures," Julian said. "Remember? You and Grandma gave them to me when I got baptized."

"Why, yes," Grandpa said, "and there's your name right on the front."

That afternoon, Grandpa taught the children how to mark important parts of the scriptures.

Grandpa said, "Be sure to read your scriptures every day."

"We will!" Julian and Lacey said. "We want to know the scriptures so we can be good missionaries."

On Sunday, the missionaries asked Lacey and Julian to invite someone to church.

"Who should we invite to come?" Julian asked Lacey.

"How about Maria and Hugo?" she replied.

When they got home, they crossed the street to Maria and Hugo's house and knocked on the door. Mrs. Sanchez, Maria and Hugo's mom, answered. "Hello, kids!"

"Hi!" Lacey said. "We came to invite you to come to church with us next week."

"Please come!" Julian said. "We're going to be in the Primary program. Will you come see us?"

Mrs. Sanchez smiled. "We would love to come."

The next Sunday, as they sang in the Primary program, Lacey and Julian smiled down at the Sanchez family, sitting by their parents.

"It's fun to invite people to church," Julian said.

When summer began, Julian and Lacey visited their aunt and uncle on their farm.

"We hear you're working on becoming good missionaries," Uncle Cecil said. "Working hard is an important part of being a good missionary."

"When we went on our missions, we worked very, very hard," Aunt Jesse said.

"So let's get to work!" Uncle Cecil said.

All week long, Julian and Lacey helped Aunt Jesse and Uncle Cecil on the farm. They learned to milk the cows early in the morning and watered all the plants in the big garden.

At the end of the week, Uncle Cecil and Aunt Jesse gave them big hugs. "You're going to be really good missionaries because you know how to work hard," Aunt Jesse said.

One day, Julian and Lacey sat on their front porch. "Look!" Julian said. "The missionaries are talking to our neighbors."

"I think it's important to talk to lots of people when you're a missionary," Lacey said.

"But it's kind of hard," Julian said. "Sometimes I get nervous."

"Then we'll just have to practice," Lacey said.

The next day, the children were walking to school. They saw Mr. Clancy pruning his bushes. "Hello!" Julian called. "You're sure working hard!"

"Hello," Mr. Clancy said. "Yes, I am. You have a good day at school, now."

A woman pushing a stroller walked toward them.

"Hello, ma'am," Lacey said. "You have a cute little girl."

The woman stopped. "Why, thank you, dear."

"I really like talking to people," Lacey said. "Let's keep practicing!"

Lacey and Julian were playing a game with their big brother, Elliott.

"Following the rules is important in our game, and it is very important when you're a missionary," Elliott said. "Good missionaries are obedient missionaries."

"How can we learn that?" Lacey asked.

"You can pay attention to the rules and the commandments all week long and do your best to obey them," Elliott replied.

All week long, the children paid attention. They kept the rules in school by raising their hands and listening to the teacher. In Primary, they learned about the commandment to pay tithing. Then they took their tithing to the bishop.

"We've been following the rules all week," Julian told Elliott.

"And it makes us really happy," Lacey added.

"We're going to be obedient missionaries when we grow up!"

The next day, Julian and Lacey visited their grandmother. "Look!" Julian said. "The missionaries!"

They stopped to talk to them. "What are you doing?" Lacey asked.

"We are helping Mrs. Welling with her yard work," the tall elder answered.

"I didn't know that missionaries did yard work!" Julian said.

The elders laughed. "Missionaries love to serve people."

"Can we help you?" Lacey asked.

"Why, sure!" the missionaries said.

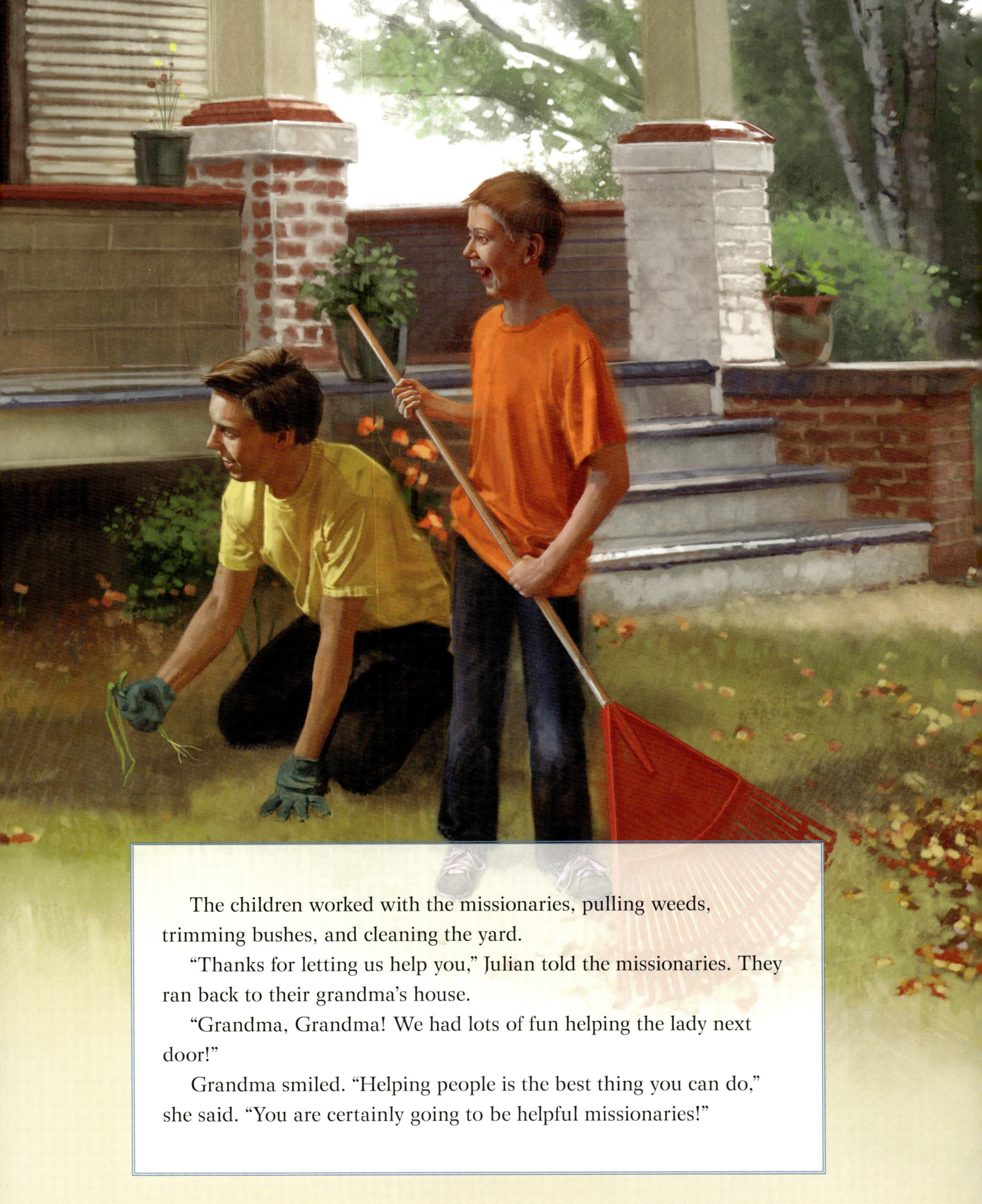

The children worked with the missionaries, pulling weeds, trimming bushes, and cleaning the yard.

"Thanks for letting us help you," Julian told the missionaries. They ran back to their grandma's house.

"Grandma, Grandma! We had lots of fun helping the lady next door!"

Grandma smiled. "Helping people is the best thing you can do," she said. "You are certainly going to be helpful missionaries!"

"When you were on your mission, what did you talk to people about?" Julian asked his brother.

"We talked about Jesus," Elliott said. "Missionaries love to talk about the Savior."

The next day at school, when Julian and Lacey were eating their lunch, their friend Alex came and sat with them.

"Hello, Alex!" Lacey said. "What did you do this weekend?"

"I went to the lake with my family. What did you do?"

"On Saturday we played soccer," Lacey said.

"And at church on Sunday we learned more about Jesus," Julian declared. "We love learning about Him."

Alex smiled.

"Talking about Jesus isn't too hard," Julian said to Lacey as they went to class.

"And it makes me feel happy," Lacey said.

"Me too," Julian replied.

"Dad, what was the hardest part of your mission?" Lacey asked as they were eating dinner.

Her father chuckled. "Elder Green, for sure. We were companions for six months. At first, he was hard to get along with. But by the end, he was my best friend."

Mother piped up. "It's important to learn to get along with other people. Your missionary companions may be from anywhere in the world. You need to learn to be patient and kind."

During the week, Lacey and Julian practiced getting along with other people.

"We were nice to Mr. Abernathy, and now he smiles and waves," Julian said.

"And I was kind to the girl who sits behind me," Lacey said.

"That's great, kids," Dad said. "Keep working on getting along with people and you'll be terrific missionaries!"

"I saw Mrs. Wallace tell the missionaries to go away," Julian told Lacey. "That made me really sad."

Lacey said, "But the missionaries keep on trying. How do they do it?"

The next Sunday, they saw the sister missionaries at church.

"How do you keep going when people tell you to go away?" Lacey asked them.

The sister missionaries smiled. "Every day we look at each other and we say, 'We will keep trying no matter what!'" Sister Lee said.

All week long, Julian and Lacey said, "We will keep trying no matter what!" while they worked on their homework and did their chores.

"I have to admit," Julian said, "when I keep trying, things work out."

"Me too," Lacey said. "Let's keep trying to keep trying!"

"Mom, what is the most important thing about being a missionary?" Lacey asked as she spread pink frosting on a sugar cookie.

"That's easy," Mom replied. "Love."

"Love?" Julian asked. "What do you mean?"

"The best missionary is like Jesus," Mom explained. "When a missionary is loving to everyone, people begin to feel loved. And then they can feel Heavenly Father's and Jesus's love for them, too."

When they finished, Lacey spoke up. "Mom, can we give these cookies to Mrs. Paretti? She's been sick a long time." Mom smiled and nodded.

Julian and Lacey ran to Mrs. Paretti's house and gave the cookies to her. "Oh, my!" she said. "A sweet treat from sweet children."

They returned home. "Mom, loving people is the best thing in the whole world," Lacey said. "Someday, I'm going to be a missionary and love everyone I meet."

"Me too," Julian said.

"You will both be wonderful missionaries," Mom said, and she gave them both a big hug.

Helps for Parents

I can look like a missionary

It is important to help children look like missionaries at a young age. This makes transitions a lot easier. Children should be taught to wear their "Sunday best" from Primary age forward. Buying a young girl a nice, modest dress and a young boy a white shirt and tie for Primary when they turn three can help them feel that they are training to become missionaries. You can refer to lds.org to see the missionary dress standards.

I can take care of myself

Training children to be independent is key in helping them prepare to be missionaries. An excellent training chart and discussion on how to do this can be found in *The Parenting Breakthrough* by Merrilee Browne Boyack (Salt Lake City: Deseret Book, 2005). Parents need to train their children to take care of themselves *before* they enter the mission field so they are ready to serve the Lord and won't have to learn those skills on their missions.

I can learn from the scriptures

A nice family tradition is to get children their own hardcover blue Book of Mormon (sold at LDS bookstores or online at store.lds.org) and have their name engraved on the front for their third birthday. Have them color inside and read from it every night. When a child is baptized, the grandparents or parents can purchase a quadruple combination of the scriptures and again have the child's name engraved. Have family home evenings about marking and using the scriptures. There are many resources at lds.org or online that can help.

I can invite others to church

Encourage children to invite their friends to church. You can even help them make invitations for family home evening and have the entire family participate in inviting others.

I can be a hard worker

Regular chores and working in the home are important preparation for missionary work. There are many resources on the Internet to help with chore charts and work assignments. As parents, we need to strengthen our children's ability to work hard and be persistent. This will help them build up the stamina and endurance they will need for missionary work.

I can talk to people

Help children practice talking to adults so they become comfortable doing so. Have them order their own food, buy movie tickets, make doctor appointments, and so forth. Encourage interaction with adults by inviting friends over, taking children to new places, and having *the children* do the talking!

I can be obedient and follow the rules

Have family home evenings about obedience, and discuss the blessings that come from keeping the commandments. Playing games and sports will also teach children to respect rules. As parents, support your children's teachers and leaders so that you model obedience to rules and standards.

Helping makes me happy

Regular service as a family is important to help children experience the joy that comes from helping others. The book *52 Weeks of Fun Family Service* by Merrilee Boyack (Salt Lake City: Deseret Book, 2007) is full of ideas to help children serve. Be sure to teach children to be kind to and patient with others who are different from them.

I like to learn and talk about Jesus

To help children testify of Christ, it can be helpful to do role-playing in family home evening. Have children practice speaking respectfully of Christ in various situations. An important aspect of missionary work is learning to feel and identify the presence of the Holy Ghost when He testifies of truth. We can help children do this as we bear our testimonies of the Savior and of the Restoration of the gospel.

I can learn to get along with other people

Many missionaries struggle in dealing with companions, new cultures, and people who are different from them. Help children prepare for this by giving them experiences in which they can interact with many kinds of people. Invite people over to your home so children can experience different cultures. You can also invite returned missionaries over for dinner or family home evening to discuss their experiences with your children.

I can keep trying no matter what

Adopt this as a motto in your home! Encourage your children to try new things and to be persistent even in the face of rejection or struggle. Having them try a new sport or musical instrument can help them learn to persevere.

I can be loving to everyone

Creating a loving heart in children takes regular effort. Identify aspects of being loving—such as kindness, patience, empathy, courtesy, and charity—and have regular family home evenings to discuss and practice these attributes. To foster these behaviors, regularly point out children's loving behavior and that of others around you. To reinforce this lesson, talk about how they *feel* when they are acting in a loving way.

It will be important that our children see *us* modeling these behaviors and sharing our love of the Savior with others so that it will be a comfortable experience for them when they become missionaries.